DREAM SOMETHING BIG

The Story of the Watts Towers

by **Dianna Hutts Aston** ♦ collages by **Susan L. Roth**

Dial Books for Young Readers
an imprint of Penguin Group (USA) Inc.

To my son, James Garrett Aston,
To Simon Rodia,
And to my friends and heroes with the gift of dyslexia:
Sergio Santana, Albert Einstein, Renee Edy, Pablo Picasso, Jay Kimball, Leonardo da Vinci,
Evelyn Chisolm DeGast, Heideloh Zieglar, Pierre Lepoureau, Keith Thompson, John F.
Kennedy, Lizzette Cuevas Santana, Mikala Harris, Thomas Edison, Alexander Graham Bell,
Chuck Collerain, Elizabeth MacQueen, Stephen Spielberg, John Lennon, Jay Leno, Henry
Ford, Richard Branson, Thomas Jefferson, Babe Ruth
—D.A.

To Leo Paul and Eva Jane with love
—S.L.R.

Artist's acknowledgements: My special thanks to Toto Aloj, Anne Athanassakis, Victoria Bond, Sharon Clifford Cresswell, Jeff Cymet, Olga Guartan, Kate Harrison, Rebecca Hoffberger (and The American Visionary Art Museum), Lauri Hornik, Virginia Kazor, Tom Koester, Lily Malcom, Alisha Niehaus, Nancy Patz, Ruth Phang, Jasmin Rubero, Susan Danza of SRS Superior Stone Inc., JAAAHLE

DIAL BOOKS FOR YOUNG READERS A division of Penguin Young Readers Group • Published by The Penguin Group • Penguin Group (USA) Inc., 375 Hudson Street, New York, NY 10014, U.S.A. • Penguin Group (Canada), 90 Eglinton Avenue East, Suite 700, Toronto, Ontario, Canada M4P 2Y3 (a division of Pearson Penguin Canada Inc.) • Penguin Books Ltd, 80 Strand, London WC2R 0RL, England • Penguin Ireland, 25 St. Stephen's Green, Dublin 2, Ireland (a division of Penguin Books Ltd) • Penguin Group (Australia), 250 Camberwell Road, Camberwell, Victoria 3124, Australia (a division of Pearson Australia Group Pty Ltd) • Penguin Books India Pvt Ltd, 11 Community Centre, Panchsheel Park, New Delhi - 110 017, India • Penguin Group (NZ), 67 Apollo Drive, Rosedale, North Shore 0632, New Zealand (a division of Pearson New Zealand Ltd) • Penguin Books (South Africa) (Pty) Ltd, 24 Sturdee Avenue, Rosebank, Johannesburg 2196, South Africa • Penguin Books Ltd, Registered Offices: 80 Strand, London WC2R 0RL, England

Text copyright © 2011 by Dianna Hutts Aston • Pictures copyright © 2011 by Susan L. Roth • Photo on page 32 courtesy of Hulton Archive/Getty Images All rights reserved • The publisher does not have any control over and does not assume any responsibility for author or third-party websites or their content • Designed by Jasmin Rubero • Text set in Cantoria MT • Manufactured in China on acid-free paper • 10 9 8 7

Aston, Dianna Hutts.
Dream something big : the story of the Watts Towers / by Dianna Hutts
Aston ; collages by Susan L. Roth.
p. cm.
Summary: In Watts, California, over a period of many years, a man known to all as Uncle Sam spends his free time collecting broken bits of pottery, glass, and other scraps and turning them into a work of art • ISBN 978-0-8037-3245-2 (hardcover) • 1. Simon Rodia's Towers (Los Angeles, Calif.)—Juvenile literature. 2.Rodia, Simon, 1879–1965—Juvenile literature. 3. Watts (Los Angeles, Calif.)—Buildings, structures, etc.—Juvenile literature. 4. Los Angeles (Calif.)—Buildings, structures, etc.—Juvenile literature. I.Roth, Susan L., ill. II. Title. NA2930.A88 2011 • [E]—dc22 • 2010028797

One chip of tile.

Uncle Sam held it in his hand, studying it,
his imagination turning like a kaleidoscope.
He put it in his pocket.

"I'm gonna do something big,"

I heard him say.

I didn't know it then, but
that single chip of tile was no longer trash.
It was the first building block
to a candy-covered castle.

Uncle Sam was my neighbor.
His name was Simon, but we never called him that.
We lived in Watts, California, on 107th Street, where
the aroma of tamales sizzled in the air, where
the trucks of Japanese farmers rumbled
to and from vegetable markets, where
music and laughter rippled
from diners and dancers at the Watts Tavern.

No one really knew what
to think about Uncle Sam,
this man who talked to himself as
he hunted through garbage heaps
for things no one wanted.
A rainbow of broken teapots, plates,
tiles, and sparkling bottles.

I collected jewels with him
along the railroad tracks—
sacks and sacks and sacks of them.
My favorites were the tiles with blue flowers,
the soda bottles with the girl and the bubbles,
and the green horse.
For every bag of bits,
he gave me a penny.
Pennies bought a lot of candy.

Uncle Sam worked in a tile factory
every day except
Sundays and holidays.
But he worked on his creation
every night,
    every Sunday,
        every holiday.
He took those bags of glass
and smashed them.

WHACK!

WHACK!

WHACK!

I watched him shove steel rods
under the railroad tracks,
and transform them into rings.
Uncle Sam was small and skinny,
but his muscles were mighty.

Some people called him crazy,
but he wasn't.
He was a *magician*.

In broken things, he saw what
no one else noticed.
He found hearts in the backs of
old ice-cream parlor chairs,
flowers in faucet handles,
the sun in rusty gears.
People who couldn't see
the hearts and flowers wondered,
Why build it?
"Why build it? I can't tell you," he said.
"Why a man make the pants?
Why a man make the shoes?"

Uncle Sam talked to himself while
he mixed a secret recipe for mortar.
"This much sand.
    This much cement.
        This much water."
Cement as powdery as flour,
sand as finely ground as sugar,
water to bind them.

He wrapped wire mesh around the poles,
smoothed the cement around them,
and carefully pressed a jigsaw of jewels
into his batter of wet cement.
Day after day,
year after year,
working on his "something big,"
without gloves, until
his fingerprints were worn away.

A ship appeared.
A tower rose.
A cactus garden bloomed.

In his strange mix of
Italian and English that was
difficult for all of us to understand,
he told us about the great towers,
and the ship he'd seen
as a child in the parades
of his village of Ribottoli.
Towers that were six stories high!

Uncle Sam worked long into the night,
singing to himself,
flitting from rung to rung like a firefly.
"Turn out the light, Uncle Sam!"
"I'm a'working up here, Marguerite!"

Every day the trains passed by with
tens of thousands of passengers a week,
going to and from Los Angeles.
The towers were Uncle Sam's stage,
the passengers his audience.
Dust from the trains swirled around him, but
he didn't let it bother him.
He was in the spotlight.

WATTS

Another tower arose.

Uncle Sam showed my children the triangles
in the branches of trees.
Triangles, he said, were
the strongest shapes, and
he built his towers with triangles.
Day after day,
year after year.

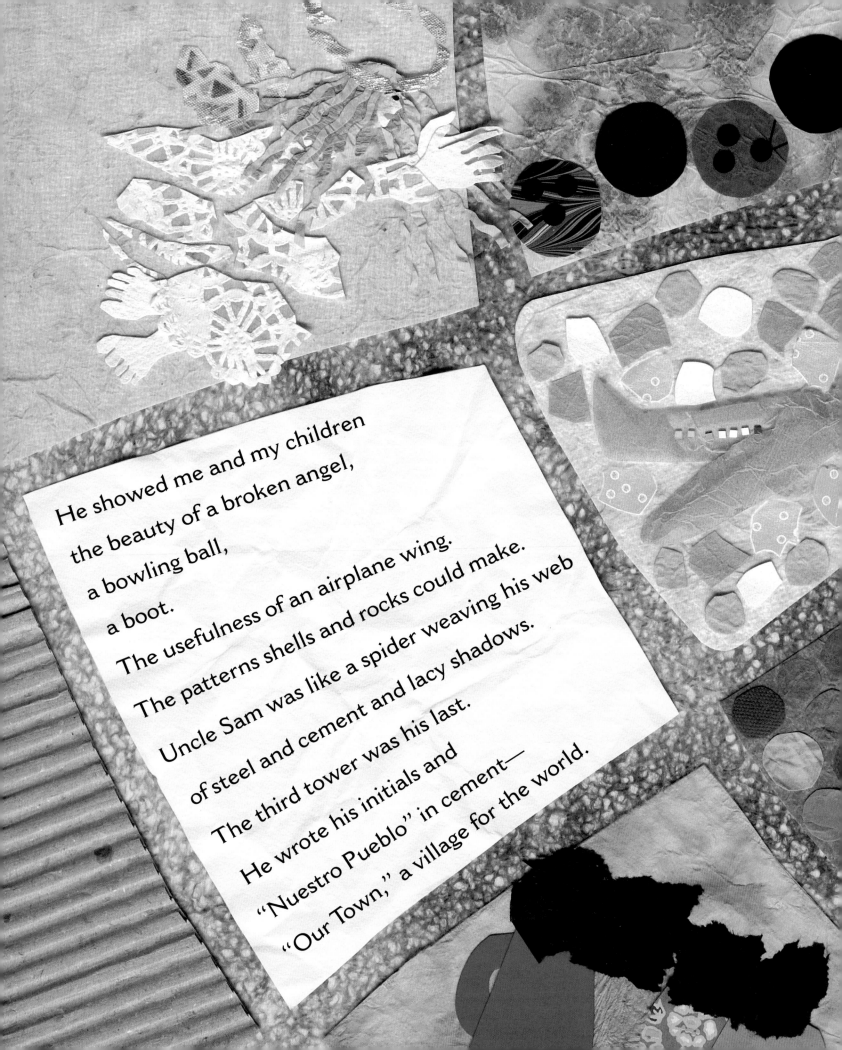

He showed me and my children
the beauty of a broken angel,
a bowling ball,
a boot.
The usefulness of an airplane wing.
The patterns shells and rocks could make.
Uncle Sam was like a spider weaving his web
of steel and cement and lacy shadows.
The third tower was his last.
He wrote his initials and
"Nuestro Pueblo" in cement—
"Our Town," a village for the world.

Not long after that, Uncle Sam suddenly
put away his tools
and jewels
and stopped building.
We were all surprised.

He put on a suit,
pinned his life savings inside it,
and gave the deed to his triangular lot—
with its ship and towers,
fountain and gardens—
to a friend and walked away.
We never saw Uncle Sam again.

But I remember him,
my uncle Sam,
my neighbor for thirty-four years,
the dreamer.

People no longer call
Simon Rodia foolish and crazy.
They call him a man of genius who built
"a gigantic flower of folk art,"
a man with a heart full of gratitude to
the country that had invited him to dream
without limits—the country that had
given him the freedom to
reach for the sky.

Uncle Sam's "something big" is
now a National Landmark.

AUTHOR'S NOTE

In his lifetime, no one ever really knew Simon Rodia. He was a mystery man, an immigrant who had sailed alone, at the age of fourteen, to the United States from Ribottoli, Italy, with a dream to do "something big."

In 1921, at the age of forty-two, Sam bought a triangular lot on 107th Street in Watts, California, a working-class community of blacks, whites, Latinos, Japanese, Germans, Greeks, and Jews. Here, Sam, the only Italian in the neighborhood, began to create what would become the Watts Towers, a fantasy of fountains, birdbaths, planters for flowers, towers, a ship, and more. Many of his neighbors didn't know what to think about a man who would salvage what others considered trash. A shy man, he couldn't read, could barely write, and spoke—often to himself—in a mix of Italian and English that was difficult to understand.

Sam built the Watts Towers without drawing plans or using a single nail, bolt, or ladder. He used simple tile-setting tools, slim steel rods called rebar, cement, wire mesh, broken bits of glass and tile, and most of all, his imagination.

The tallest of the towers stands 99.5 feet high (30.34 meters). The central tower stands 97.8 feet high (29.83 meters), and the east tower 55 feet high (16.76 meters). The ship, built in honor of one of his heroes, a thirteenth-century explorer named Marco Polo, has a spire of 28 feet.

99.5 feet high →

97.8 feet high →

55 feet high →

In 1955, thirty-four years after he had first begun, Sam declared his creation complete and gave the deed to the property to a neighbor. The mysterious Sam abruptly left for Martinez, California, where his sister and her family lived. He never saw the towers again. He died in 1965 at the age of eighty-six.

A child once asked Sam why he had built the towers. "To make a pretty scenery, I think. And make that place famous."

Thanks to the Watts Tower Arts Center staff for their contributions.

6,000 bits of glass

10,000 seashells

15,000 tiles

11,000 pieces of pottery

Create your own Watts Tower

You might not own a plot of land in Watts, California, but don't let that stop you from building your own Watts Tower! All you need are some beads, buttons, and pipe cleaners to represent the tiles, shells, glass, and wire that Uncle Sam used to construct his towers.

But before you can begin, you need to find something extra-special that inspires you. You need that one piece of tile, or that one bead or button, that makes *you* dream something big. Uncle Sam's towers all started with a piece of tile he found on the street. So try going outside to find your inspiration. Grab your parents' hands and take them for a Dream Walk, and then look for something special to put on your tower. Talk about your dreams while you search—and who knows? Maybe your mom used to want to be an archeologist too!

You will need:

Pipe cleaners or florist's wire

Magazine clippings

Squares of florist's sponge foam or craft foam

Assorted foam shapes

Assorted beads and buttons

Glue

Get a Little Help from Your Friends!
Uncle Sam knew that people can't always make a dream come true by themselves. They need a community of friends and family to help them achieve it. Uncle Sam loved his community, and in return, they protected his towers long after he disappeared. When the city of Los Angeles tried to knock down the Watts Towers, the people of Los Angeles County fought to keep them standing. In honor of the community effort that kept Uncle Sam's dream alive, try building your tower with friends—together you can dream up something much bigger than you could by yourself!

1

Push pipe cleaners or florist's wire into the foam base.

2

String beads, buttons, and foam shapes along pipe cleaners or florist's wire.

3

Bend pipe cleaners together or wrap them around the florist's wire.

4

Repeat until you've made fun, intricate towers.

5

Tear inspiring magazine images into small pieces.

6

Glue the ripped pieces or foam shapes to the foam base.

7

Allow to dry.